Chow Chow
Publishing

This Chow Chow book belongs to:

For Savanna and Malaika – S.H.

For Bianka and Bernadett – B.B.

First published in Great Britain in 2024 by Chow Chow Publishing

Disclaimer: although the majority of spiders in the UK are non-venomous, this is not neccessarily the case elsewhere in the world and caution is always recommended when handling spiders. The author takes no liability for any possible harm done by the handling of spiders.

ISBN 978-1-06-863390-4 (paperback)

ISBN 978-1-06-863391-1 (hardcover)

A CIP catalogue record for this book is available from the British Library.

www.chowchowpublishing.co.uk

www.artstation.com/bettinab

MY NEW FRIEND
SUNNY THE SPIDER

written by
Silke Haack

illustrated by
Bettina Brasko

It was just an ordinary evening and I was gettin

... but what was that dark moving

Mum came and threw it out the window.
"Done," she said, "you can relax.
What's the big deal with them anyway, Tim?"

"Look at them Mum, they are so creepy... the way they sit still and then all of a sudden start to run. They are too unpredictable, they have too many legs and they're too fast — THAT'S the big deal!" "Alright," said Mum with a smile, "sweet dreams my Love."

But instead of going to sleep

I was up for a while, thinking about spiders...

How I wish they didn't look so scary,
their fat bodies all creepy and hairy.
And I wish they didn't munch on a fly,
to say that's not revolting would be a lie,
and who needs a fly when there are sweets to buy?

A bit of colour surely wouldn't hurt,
yes, a bright coloured spider eating lemon curd,
just a few simple swaps would change my mind,
perhaps – if that was the case – I could be kind.

Eventually, I started feeling tired.
What I didn't realise though is
while I snuggled up all cosy in my bed...

... the spider outside felt very very sad...

How I wish humans could see my true colours,
outside I'm just grey – but inside I have others.
And I wish they wouldn't scream and shout,
hit me, spray me and throw me out,
why can't they be a more loving and considerate crowd?

A bit of thoughtfulness surely wouldn't hurt,
then we'd hang out together sharing some lemon curd.
Yes, a happy, jolly human being
is what I'd most dearly love seeing.

And as hopeful as can be
the spider closed its eyes and went to sleep.

The next morning I had all forgotten about the spider.
As usual I got myself ready for school, but then,
when I opened the front door, I got the
BIGGEST SURPRISE EVER!

There, in our front garden, sat an enormous, colourful spider. You would expect me to scream, but the funny thing is, it didn't actually look the tiniest bit scary. It looked ... well ... kind of cute... more like a gigantic, cuddly soft toy.

I know,' he said and his face lifted.
I have no idea what happened, but –
here we are – would you like a ride to school?"

I hesitated for a moment, but then walked over to him, took a deep breath and pulled myself up.

He started walking and that was nice, but as he sped up
my tummy began to tickle. It made me giggle at first,
but that giggle soon turned into a big laugh and finally –
I couldn't help it – I was cheering 'WOOHOOO!'
I absolutely loved it! It was the coolest thing on earth!

"Pick you up later?" Sunny asked as we reached the school.

"That'd be amazing!" I responded and walked into the building, where my friends bombarded me with questions.

The whole school turned into a big chitter-chatter. We tried to do some maths and English, but no one could focus, not even Mrs Teddington, our teacher. Everyone was just waiting to meet my cool new friend – Sunny the Spider.

When the bell rang, everyone ran outside to meet Sunny.

"How about some ice cream?" he suggested.

"I thought you eat flies..." I responded.

"Not when there are sweets to buy!" he said with a wink.

and so we went and got
ourselves a scoop of ice cream
and headed to the park.

Sunny said he'd never been to a playground before and I was so excited to take him.

"Let's go on the slide I called and slid down with a 'wheeee', but when I turned around I saw Sunny sitting at the top, looking unsure

He leaned forward ...

... but as he started to slide his legs got all tumbled up, and he couldn't hold on to his ice cream any longer, which now slid in front of him with Sunny toppling behind and landing in it face forward with a BUMP!

"Are you ok?" I gasped worriedly. Sunny burst into laughter. "That was so much fun!" he said, "But aww, my ice cream!" "Don't worry," I told him, "we've got some lemon curd at home. Come on, Mum will be waiting for me."

Mum said Sunny could stay for tea, so we all sat together digging into yummy pizza. "Mum," I asked, "where is Sunny going to live, now that he's giant?"

"I suppose he can live with us if he likes?" Sunny nodded with a huge grin on his face.

"Sunny, I know I was really unkind yesterday, I'm sorry! I do understand now that everyone has feelings – even spiders – and I will be your friend regardless of whether you stay big or return to being small."

"Thank you Tim, apology accepted," he said in his happiest voice.

"Bedtime boys," Mum called,
so Sunny and I got ready
and Mum read us a lovely story.
"Sweet dreams you two," she said as she turned off the light.
"Good night Tim," Sunny yawned. "Night night Sunny, looking
forward to the adventures we will have tomorrow."